For my family. Lori. Amelie.
and Madaline —N.K.

For David —B.B.

Printed in Malaysia
First Edition, October 2015
10 9 8 7 6 5 4 3 2 1
FAC-029191-15156
Designed by Scott Piehl
Reinforced binding
Library of Congress Catalog Card Number: 2014953574
ISBN 978-1-4231-5732-8

CLOUD COUNTRY

CONCEPT AND PICTURES BY **Noah Klocek**

WORDS BY **Bonny Becker**

DISNEP HYPERION

Los Angeles · New York

GALE

floated on a warm breeze,
watching the Land Below.

Far off, a deer trotted across a meadow.
Ducklings scrambled after their mother.

Gale sighed, wishing she could look at
the world like this forever.

"Earth-gazing again?" asked her mother.
Gale nodded. She knew she should have been
practicing her cloud shapes.

Today was Formation School Graduation Day,
when all the young cloudlets like Gale would show
the Guardians what cloud shapes they could make.

Already, other cloudlets and their families
were swiftly floating by. Gale couldn't help noticing
how well they drifted and billowed.

Though she had been practicing all year,
she couldn't make even one real cloud shape.
She closed her eyes tightly and tried again.

She thought dark, stormy thoughts.

"Does this look like a cumulonimbus cloud?"
she asked her little brother, Nimba.

"Elephant cloud!"
he cried.

Gale thought puffy, fluffy, fat-cheeked thoughts,
hoping to create a cumulus cloud.

"Lamb cloud!"
Nimba clapped his hands.

"Don't worry," Momma said.
"I know you can do it, Gale."

She hoped Momma was right!

It would be wonderful to graduate from Formation
School, forming a cloud shape she could be proud of.
But Gale was out of time to practice. The other cloudlets
in Gale's class were moving onto the stage.

The Guardians called each student forward one by one.
Cirree's cloud stretched into a wispy stratus. Strato's
cloud rose into a wide altocumulus and disappeared.
Bluster's cloud whirled around and around.
Everyone knew he wanted to make
funnel clouds when he grew up.

Soon it was Gale's turn.

"Formation?" asked the head Guardian.

"Cumulus cloud," she mumbled.

Her stomach felt full of tiny slivers of lightning.
But Gale took a deep breath and thought
plump, floaty cumulus thoughts.

"Tugboat?" guessed the head Guardian.
Quickly, Gale tried again. She thought fierce,
flashing cumulonimbus thoughts.

"Dog?" another Guardian guessed.
They were looking at each other now,
and Gale could hear everyone else murmuring.

"Would you like to try once more?"
the head Guardian asked.

Gale couldn't help it: she began to rain.

Raindrops pitter-pattered down her cheeks.

She had spent too much time looking

at the Land Below after all!

The head Guardian tried again.
"No other formations?" he asked.

"No," Gale whispered. "Just things like mountains
and bears and frogs." The crowd gasped.

"Only Land Below shapes?" asked the oldest Guardian.

Gale nodded. She could see Momma's worried face.
The Guardians bent their heads to talk.

Finally, the oldest Guardian knelt beside her.

"We are so glad to finally find you."

His voice was gentle. "We've been waiting for another

Daydream Cloud for a long time."

"Daydream Cloud?" Gale had never heard of that.

"You will make fish and boats,
waterfalls and crows,"
said the head Guardian.

"You'll make castles in the air!"
said another.

Gale was confused.
"I'd make my own shapes?"
she asked.

The oldest Guardian laughed.
"That's what Daydream Clouds do.
They make shapes from the Land Below.
Shapes the world can dream on."

"Congratulations, class,"
the head Guardian announced.
"You all have graduated from Formation School!"

Gale could hardly believe it.

She would be allowed to earth-gaze all day!

She could create shapes of the many things she loved.

The swaying trees,

the lumbering bears,

the great fish.

Gale twirled so fast she nearly
made a funnel cloud!

Gale's mother hugged her.

"I'm so proud of you."

Nimba reached for her hand.

"Gale happy?"

Gale nodded, and she thought happy, puffy thoughts.

Not because she was trying to make a cumulus cloud . . .

. . . but because she believed that happy,
puffy thoughts would make the best shapes
for the Land Below to dream on.